Monster Mountain

Thunderbelle's Flying Machine

For Oscar Birkbeck
K.W.
For Sonny and Nia,
with love
G. P-R.

First published in 2007 by Orchard Books
First paperback publication in 2008

ORCHARD BOOKS
338 Euston Road, London NW1 3BH
Orchard Books Australia
Level 17/207 Kent St, Sydney, NSW 2000

ISBN 978 1 84362 622 0 (hardback)
ISBN 978 1 84362 630 5 (paperback)

1 3 5 7 9 10 8 6 4 2 (hardback)
1 3 5 7 9 10 8 6 4 2 (paperback)

Printed in China

Orchard Books is a division of Hachette Children's Books,
an Hachette Livre UK company.

www.orchardbooks.co.uk

Monster Mountain

Thunderbelle's Flying Machine

Karen Wallace

Illustrated by

Guy Parker-Rees

ORCHARD BOOKS

"I want to fly," said Thunderbelle.
"I want to look down and see my
house from the sky."

"But you're a monster," said
Clodbuster. "Monsters don't fly."

"Pipsquawk can fly," said
Thunderbelle.
"But she's half bat," said
Clodbuster.

Thunderbelle didn't answer. She
made herself some wings.

She pulled the straps and the wings
went up and down. She pulled
harder and harder and the wings
flapped faster and faster. But
nothing happened.

"What have I done wrong?" cried
Thunderbelle.
Clodbuster scratched his head.
"Maybe they have to be bat wings."

Thunderbelle rang the Brilliant Ideas gong. **Bong! Bong! Bong!**

The other monsters came as fast
as they could. Roxorus skidded by
on his skateboard.

Mudmighty slid down on
a cabbage leaf.

Pipsquawk landed on a low
branch.

"What's the brilliant idea?" cried
Roxorus.

"I want to fly!" cried Thunderbelle.

"What about a giant catapult?"
said Mudmighty.

"What happens when I land?"
asked Thunderbelle.
"A great big BUMP!" said
Mudmighty.

"That's not a brilliant idea," said
Thunderbelle.

"What about a cannon?" cried
Clodbuster.

Pipsquawk flapped down from
her branch.

"We'll build you an aeroplane!"

Thunderbelle jumped up and down
and the ground shook.
"Pipsquawk, you're a genius!"

A Thunderbelle-sized aeroplane
would need to be very big.
All the monsters offered to help.

Roxorus found round
stones for the wheels.

Clodbuster brought wood
and a pot of paint
from his house.

Mudmighty picked beetroot
leaves for the wings.
Thunderbelle liked the
pink bits in them.

Pipsquawk collected sticks and
feathers and pieces of shell.
All morning the monsters
hammered and
glued and painted.

Thunderbelle went to make them
some lunch.
When she came back, she nearly
dropped her tray of strawberry jam
sandwiches.

There was a really cool aeroplane
in her garden!

After lunch, Thunderbelle put on
a flying suit, a helmet and a pair
of goggles. She sat in the pilot's
seat.

"It's easy," said Clodbuster.
"All you do is push the shell, flip
the stick and twirl the feather.
Then, VROOM! You're off!"

Thunderbelle didn't move.
"What's wrong?" shouted
the others.

"I forgot I'm afraid of heights!"
Thunderbelle wailed.

The other monsters didn't know
what to say.
Everyone had worked so hard on
the aeroplane.

"Don't cry, Thunderbelle," said
Pipsquawk.
"Anyone can be afraid of heights."
"What am I going to do-o-o-o?"
wailed Thunderbelle.

Pipsquawk swung back and forth
and thought hard.
"I know what to do!" she squawked.
"We'll turn the aeroplane into
a swing!"

First Pipsquawk found
the perfect tree.

Then Mudmighty pulled
up some vines.

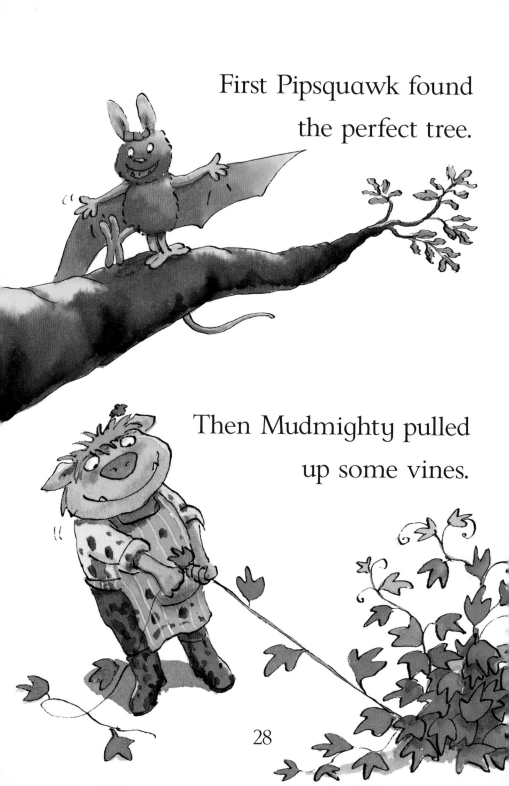

Clodbuster and Roxorus
made two thick ropes.

At last they hung the aeroplane
from the tree. The swing
was ready!

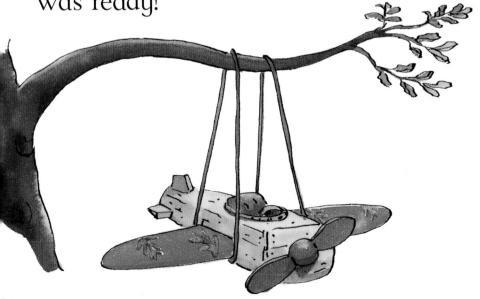

Thunderbelle climbed into the
pilot's seat.
The other monsters gave her
a great big PUSH!

Thunderbelle soared into the air
and whooped with joy.
"My aeroplane is the best
swing ever!"

Monster Mountain

All priced at £8.99. Monster Mountain books are available from
all good bookshops, or can be ordered direct from the publisher:
Orchard Books, PO BOX 29, Douglas IM99 1BQ. Credit card orders
please telephone 01624 836000 or fax 01624 837033 or visit our website:
www.orchardbooks.co.uk or e-mail: bookshop@enterprise.net for details.

To order please quote title, author and ISBN and your full name and address.
Cheques and postal orders should be made payable to 'Bookpost plc.'
Postage and packing is FREE within the UK
(overseas customers should add £2.00 per book).

Prices and availability are subject to change.